HOCUS POCUS HOTEL

Hocus Pocus Hotel is published by Stone Arch Books
A Capstone Imprint
1710 Roe Crest Dr.
North Mankato, Minnesota 56003
www.capstonepub.com

Cataloging-in-Publication Data is available at the Library
of Congress website.

ISBN: 978-1-4342-6508-1 (library binding)

Summary: Charlie finds himself on the hidden 13th
floor of the Abracadabra Hotel. He discovers both Tyler
and the magician Brack. Brack was trapped there by a
mysterious figure he could not identify.

Photo credits: Shutterstock
Abracadabra Hotel illustration: Brann Garvey
Designed by Kristi Carlson

Printed in China.
092013
007733LEOS14